# THE DONKEY AND THE ROCK

To Tsering Tashi
Deputy Secretary/Press Officer to His Holiness the Dalai Lama, with gratitude

The tale of the donkey and the rock is said to have originated in India in 550 B.C., with the Buddha acting as the judge and instructing his disciples to avoid foolish curiosity. Humor and wisdom gave the tale broad appeal, and it spread throughout Asia in many variations. One particularly famous version was written in China in the eighteenth century. It was entitled "Cheng Ban Qiao Tries a Rock."* Cheng Ban Qiao was a celebrated painter, writer, and magistrate of the time. Today, however, the story is often heard in Tibet. My version was told to me by my Chinese Buddhist husband, Tze-si Huang, who remembers hearing it from his grandmother when he was growing up in Wildcat Stream, near Chungking, in China's Sichuan Province.

*Adapted by Huan Shi Ming and published by Morning Glory Press, Beijing, 1986.

Henry Holt and Company, Inc., *Publishers since 1866*, 115 West 18th Street, New York, New York 10011
Henry Holt is a registered trademark of Henry Holt and Company, Inc. Copyright © 1999 by Demi. All rights reserved.
Published in Canada by Fitzhenry & Whiteside Ltd., 195 Allstate Parkway, Markham, Ontario L3R 4T8.
Library of Congress Cataloging-in-Publication Data
Demi. The donkey and the rock / Demi. Summary: In this version of a tale with many Asian variations, a wise king, who rules a town full of foolish people in the mountains of Tibet, puts a donkey and a rock on trial to settle the dispute between two honest men. [1. Folklore—China—Tibet.] I. Title. PZ8.1.D38Do 1999 398.2'0951'502—dc21 [E] 98-14743

ISBN 0-8050-5959-8 / First Edition—1999. Printed in the United States of America on acid-free paper. ∞
The artist used gouache and ink on vellum and watercolor washes to create the illustrations for this book. 10 9 8 7 6 5 4 3 2 1

# THE DONKEY AND THE ROCK

## DEMI

Henry Holt and Company
New York

A long time ago, in the land of Tibet, with mountains so high they seemed to touch the sky, there was a king who was an honored and a just man. From the tallest mountains to the deepest valleys he was known for his fair judgment.

On a mountain ruled by this wise king lived two poor men.
Each man was good and honest and did the best he could to
support his ten children, wife, mother, father, uncles, and aunts.

One day one of the men started walking to a village with his ten children playing and dancing along the way. The man was carrying a jar of oil and selling the oil as he went. Soon, the man grew tired and set his jar of oil on a rock while he rested.

As he lay there, his neighbor came down the
mountain, with his ten children playing and dancing
along the way, driving his donkey in front of him.

The donkey was covered with a huge pile of wood so that he looked like a little mountain himself. The poor donkey didn't see the jar of oil sitting on the rock. As he went past the jar, he knocked it off, breaking it into a million pieces and splashing oil all over the place.

The man who owned the oil was very, very angry.
He blamed the donkey's owner. The donkey's owner
said he wasn't the one who should be blamed. The
donkey should be blamed.

The man with the oil said it was all he had in
the world to sell for food for his ten children and
his wife and his mother and father and his uncles
and aunts. It wasn't his fault the jar was broken!

Both men shouted and quarreled and argued and jumped up and down. Their ten children shouted and quarreled and argued and jumped up and down. Finally, since no one could agree, the men decided to go to the king for help.

The king questioned them carefully about the matter and decided that neither man was to blame. They were both good and honest men who took great care of their ten children, wives, mothers, fathers, uncles, and aunts. Since neither one was to blame, the fault must lie with either the donkey or the rock.

The king sent his men to arrest the donkey and the rock. The poor little donkey was locked up with chains around his neck. The king's men captured the rock and wrapped chains around it, too.

Soon news of this peculiar case had spread throughout the kingdom.

When the children, wives, mothers, fathers, uncles, and aunts heard that their great king had arrested a donkey and a rock, they thought he had surely gone crazy.

The king announced that the case
would be tried the next morning. A
great procession was held with flags
and banners, trumpets and cymbals.

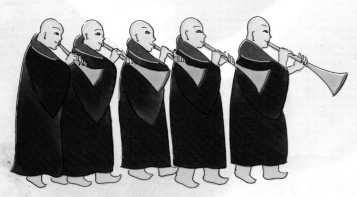

The idea that a donkey and a rock could have
a trial in court made no sense to anyone. But
curious to see such a bizarre spectacle, people
rushed to the courtyard.

The king arrived and took his seat. Then he instructed his guards to shut and lock all the gates.

Finally, the trial
was about to begin.

The king said, "As you know, there is no law by which to judge a donkey and a rock. So why have you come to see such an absurd thing? Now, because of your silly curiosity, each of you must pay ten coins before you may leave."

The people, looking very ashamed of themselves but glad to be freed, handed over their money and slipped through the gates. After the last coin had been collected, the king gave all the money to the man who had lost his oil. The donkey was freed, the rock was returned, and the court was closed. Both men went home happy.

The king continued to rule the land justly and wisely, and from that day on the people tried not to let idle curiosity get the better of them.

And they never forgot the lesson they learned from the trial of the donkey and the rock.